My First SHARED READING

I Can Read!

Pete the Kitty
AND
THE THREE
BEARS

by Kimberly
& James Dean

HARPER

An Imprint of HarperCollins Publishers

ONCE UPON A TIME . . .

Pete the Kitty walked
to the woods.
Pete saw a house.

"Hello? Anybody home?"
asked Pete.

No one was home.

Something smelled yummy.

Pete saw three pizzas.

The first pizza was too hot.

The second pizza was too cold.

The last pizza was just right!

It was dynamite!

Pete ate the pizza.

Yummy!

Then Pete saw three guitars.
"Let's jam!" Pete said.

The first guitar was too loud.

The second guitar was too quiet.

The last guitar was just right!
It was out-of-sight!

Pete rocked out.

Oops! The string broke.

Then Pete felt sleepy.

He wanted to take a nap.

The first bed was too hard.

The second bed was too soft.

The last bed was just right.
Nighty night!

Pete fell asleep.

Papa, Mama, and Baby Bear
came home.
Someone ate their pizza.

"Mine is all gone,"
said Baby Bear.

Someone played their guitars.
"Mine is broken,"
said Baby Bear.

Someone slept in their beds.

"They're still in my bed,"

said Baby Bear.

The three bears growled.

Pete woke up.

Baby Bear was crying.

Pete felt bad that he ate
the bears' pizza.

Pete felt bad he played
their guitars.

Pete felt bad he slept
in their beds.

Pete knew what to say.
"I am sorry I didn't ask
to use your stuff," Pete said.

"Everyone makes mistakes,"
Mama Bear said.
"We forgive you, Pete,"
Papa Bear said.

Pete fixed the guitar.

Baby Bear was happy.

"Let's be friends, Pete,"
Baby Bear said.

The new friends rocked out.

It was just right!